For my mom and dad—D. J. M.

For Mia and Ruby—J. K.

A FEIWEL AND FRIENDS BOOK

An Imprint of Macmillan

MONSTERGARTEN. Text copyright © 2013 by Daniel J. Mahoney. Illustrations copyright © 2013 by Jef Kaminsky.
All rights reserved. Printed in China by South China Printing Co. Ltd., Dongguan City, Guangdong Province.
For information, address Feiwel and Friends, 175 Fifth Avenue, New York, N.Y. 10010.

Library of Congress Cataloging-in-Publication Data Available

ISBN: 978-1-250-01441-2

Book design by Rich Deas and Véronique Lefèvre Sweet

Feiwel and Friends logo designed by Filomena Tuosto

The artwork was created in Corel Painter using a "digital" piece of soft vine charcoal to draw
the black lines and paint the colors. Final color paintings were exported to Adobe Photoshop
and page layout was done in InDesign.

First Edition: 2013

1 3 5 7 9 10 8 6 4 2

mackids.com

MONSTERGARTEN

Story by **Daniel J. Mahoney**   Pictures by **Jef Kaminsky**

Feiwel and Friends
NEW YORK

"Did I **scare** you?"

"Um, no. Not really," said Kevin.

"Not even a little bit?" Patrick asked.

"Nope," Kevin replied.

"I'm in **big** trouble then, because I have to be scary by **tomorrow**," said Patrick. "It's one of the rules for going into Monstergarten. A first-grader told me."

"Well, you came to the right place," said Kevin. "I'm an **expert** at being scary. I bet I'll be the scariest kid in the whole class! You just need a little practice."

"I think you're ready," Kevin said. "Try giving Snowball a scare."

"Maybe we should try something else," said Kevin.

"Let's go to my house and spy on my sister and her friend," Kevin said. "I'm an **expert** at being scary, but those girls are **really scary!**"

"RRRRAAAAHHHH-RRR!"

"Oooh! So scary, we forgot to scream!" the girls cried.

Kevin took Patrick to his room.
"I know where to get some good ideas for the
first day of Monstergarten," Kevin told his friend.

The boys looked at pictures of scary monsters.
"Just do what they're doing," Kevin suggested.

Patrick knew there were things that should come to him naturally.

Like SHOWING HIS CLAWS,

and GROWLING.

FLASHING HIS FANGS,

and **RAISING HIS ARMS.**

But, in what order? What was the **right** way for him to be **scary**?

"Are you ready for the first day of Monstergarten?"
Patrick asked Kevin.

"Of course," said Kevin. "I'm an expert at being scary,
remember? You just need a little more practice."

That evening before dinner,
Patrick practiced.

And practiced.

"Tomorrow's the big day, buddy!" said
Patrick's dad. "Your first day of Monstergarten!"

"Is everything all right, honey?" his mother asked.
"You didn't eat your lizardloaf."

At bedtime, Patrick's mother laid out his new backpack.

"What if I don't like my teacher?" Patrick asked.
"What if I have to go to the bathroom? What if I'm not scary enough?"

His mother gave him a hug.
"It'll be fine," she whispered.
"Just be YOURSELF."

The next day, all the new monstergartners kissed their parents good-bye and headed into their new classroom. They met their teacher, Mr. Goop.

Everyone was ready to start their day. Well, almost everyone . . .

"Whoa, Patrick! You scared me! You're probably the scariest kid in our whole class!"

"Really?" Patrick asked.

"Totally," Kevin replied.

"Thanks, Kevin. I couldn't have done it without you."

"I LOVE MONSTERGARTEN!" said Kevin.

"Yeah. It's super-scary," said Patrick.